Austria

JOHN PERRITANO

www.av2books.com

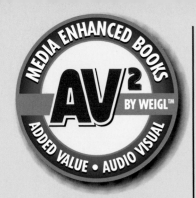

MEDIA ENHANCED BOOKS
AV²
BY WEIGL™
ADDED VALUE · AUDIO VISUAL

AV² provides enriched content that supplements and complements this book. Weigl's AV² books strive to create inspired learning and engage young minds in a total learning experience.

Your AV² Media Enhanced books come alive with...

Audio
Listen to sections of the book read aloud.

Key Words
Study vocabulary, and complete a matching word activity.

Video
Watch informative video clips.

Quizzes
Test your knowledge.

Embedded Weblinks
Gain additional information for research.

Slideshow
View images and captions, and prepare a presentation.

Try This!
Complete activities and hands-on experiments.

... and much, much more!

Go to **www.av2books.com**, and enter this book's unique code.

BOOK CODE

AVS73495

AV² by Weigl brings you media enhanced books that support active learning.

Published by AV² by Weigl
350 5th Avenue, 59th Floor
New York, NY 10118
Website: www.av2books.com

Library of Congress Control Number: 2019938446

ISBN 978-1-7911-0902-8 (hardcover)
ISBN 978-1-7911-0903-5 (softcover)
iSBN 978-1-7911-0904-2 (multi-user eBook)
iSBN 978-1-7911-0905-9 (single-user eBook)

Printed in Guangzhou, China
1 2 3 4 5 6 7 8 9 0 23 22 21 20 19

062019
311018

Editor Heather Kissock
Art Director Terry Paulhus
Layout: Tammy West

Photo Credits
Every reasonable effort has been made to trace ownership and to obtain permission to reprint copyright material. The publishers would be pleased to have any errors or omissions brought to their attention so that they may be corrected in subsequent printings.

Weigl acknowledges Getty Images, Alamy, Newscom, iStock, Wikimedia, and Shutterstock as its primary photo suppliers for this title.

Contents

Austria Overview

Located in central Europe, Austria is a country known for its scenic mountains, crystal lakes, and winding Danube River. Once a great **empire**, Austria was for centuries one of the most dominant forces in Europe. It reached the height of its power in the 1500s. At that time, its ruling family, the Habsburgs, controlled a vast amount of territory, stretching from Austria to Spain. Over the next 400 years, the empire gradually declined before collapsing in 1918, at the end of World War I. From the gnarled ruins, a new, modern Austria emerged—a country that is today one of the most prosperous in the world.

Austrian Christmas markets are popular with residents and tourists alike. They start in mid-November and remain open until the end of the year.

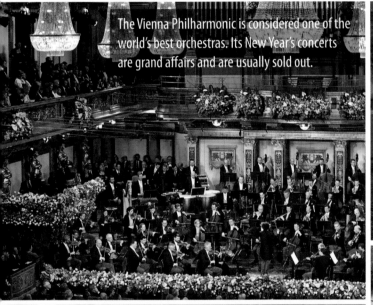

The Vienna Philharmonic is considered one of the world's best orchestras. Its New Year's concerts are grand affairs and are usually sold out.

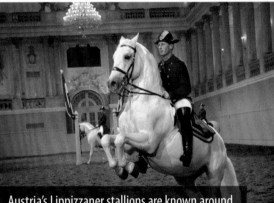

Austria's Lippizzaner stallions are known around the world for their beauty and intricate footwork.

Schnitzel is a traditional Austrian dish. Made from veal, it is often served with lingonberries and a slice of lemon.

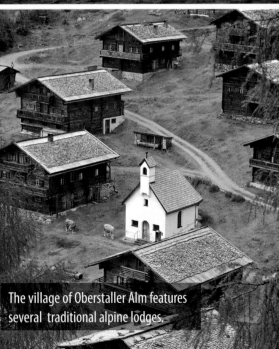

The village of Oberstaller Alm features several traditional alpine lodges.

Exploring Austria

Austria is a land-locked nation, surrounded by eight countries. Switzerland and Liechtenstein lie to the west. Germany borders Austria to the northwest, while the Czech **Republic** is to north. Slovakia and Hungary border on the east. Italy and Slovenia lie to the south. Austria covers an area of 32,386 square miles (83,879 square kilometers). It extends a distance of approximately 360 miles (579 km) from east to west.

Danube River

Germany

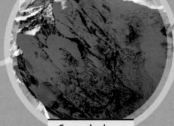

Grossglockner

Switzerland

Liechtenstein

N

Map Legend

 Austria

 Land

 Water

Bohemian Massif

▲ Grossglockner

Danube River

📍 Capital City

SCALE

250 Miles

250 Kilometers

Grossglockner

Austria boasts some of the highest peaks in the Alps. The Grossglockner, or "black mountain," rises 12,460 feet (3,798 meters) above sea level and is the tallest peak in the Eastern Alps.

Czech Republic

Bohemian Massif

Vienna

Bohemian Massif

Vienna

AUSTRIA

Hungary

Italy

Slovenia

Croatia

Danube River

At a length of 1,770 miles (2,850 km), the Danube is Europe's second-longest river, after the Volga. It serves as a vital travel and trade route, linking Austria's largest cities with northern and central Europe.

Vienna

With about 1.8 million residents, Vienna is Austria's capital and largest city. The city is a cultural hub. It is well-known for its architecture, museums, concerts, and cuisine.

Bohemian Massif

Covering approximately 10 percent of the country's land, the Bohemian Massif is located in Austria's north. The rolling landscape of this plateau is known for its forests and granite base.

LAND AND CLIMATE

Lake Constance traverses a length of 40 miles (64 km) and measures 7.5 miles (12 km) across at its widest point.

Austria teems with high mountain peaks, deep lakes, and evergreen forests. The Alps run through the center of the country from west to east, forming a natural barrier between northern and southern Europe. **Geologists** subdivide the Alps into northern and southern ranges. However, the highest peaks are found in the Central Alps. Most of this area is covered by large **glaciers**.

Austria is also home to many glacial lakes, most of which were formed about 2.6 million to 12,000 years ago. Austria's largest lakes lay partly in the territory of other countries. Lake Constance, with a surface area of 208 square miles (539 sq. km), straddles the borders between Austria, Germany, and Switzerland. Austria shares Neusiedler Lake, which covers 122 square miles (316 sq. km), with Hungary.

The Danube is Austria's most important waterway. All of the country's rivers and streams flow into it, each carrying glacial melt from high in the Alps. Some of the better-known rivers in Austria include the Enns, Drava, and Traun.

The Vienna Basin covers an area nearly 120 miles (193 km) long and 37 miles (60 km) wide. Located in the eastern part of the country, this lowland area separates the Alps from the West Carpathian Mountains. The basin is known to have some of Austria's best farmland.

In general, Austria has a temperate climate. There is, however, variance between regions. In the north, the climate is mild, with rainy winters and humid summers. Southern Austria is dominated by a Mediterranean climate. Summers here are hot and dry. Winters are mild and rainy. Mountainous areas can experience low temperatures and heavy snowfall during the winter.

The Tannheim Valley is located in the Allgäu Alps, a range located in the northern part of the country, near the German border.

PLANTS AND ANIMALS

Nearly two-thirds of Austria is covered by forests and meadows. Spruce are the dominant trees, but oak, beech, and larch are also numerous. Most of the country's coniferous trees are found in the foothills and areas of higher elevation. Broad-leaved deciduous trees are more abundant in the lowlands, where it is warmer.

Austria is also home to a flower called edelweiss. This star-shaped plant grows in mountainous areas, at altitudes as high as 8,860 feet (2,700 m). Known as the queen flower, it is Austria's national flower. Other wildflowers growing in the Austrian mountains include heather and the alpine rose.

A wide range of wildlife can be found in Austria. Birds such as storks, cranes, owls, and buzzards soar the skies. Deer, ibexes, and brown bears are some of the larger mammals found roaming the land. Smaller mammals include martens, rabbits, groundhogs, and foxes. The country's lakes and rivers brim with rainbow trout, pike, perch, grayling, and carp.

Alpine ibexes typically live along the snowline of the European Alps. They can be found at elevations up to 15,000 feet (4,600 m).

NATURAL RESOURCES

44% Portion of Austria covered by forests.

10th Austria's rank among world producers of graphite.

60% Portion of Austria's electricity generated by hydroelectric plants.

Austria's mountains, forests, rivers, and lakes provide the country with an abundance of natural resources. The country is one of the world's largest producers of magnesite, a mineral used in the chemical industry. Austria also produces about 2.5 percent of the world's graphite, which is used to make pencils. The country ranks 11th in the world for the production of talc. This soft mineral is used to make baby powder and other products. Other minerals found in Austria include iron ore, gypsum, quartz, and salt.

Austria uses its fast-moving rivers and streams to produce **hydroelectricity**. The country has approximately 3,800 hydropower plants. Other energy resources found within the country include natural gas and petroleum.

Timber and wood products are also important natural resources for the country. Austria has 9.6 million acres (3.9 million hectares) of forested land. Approximately 7.7 million acres (3.1 million ha) are used for commercial purposes.

Located in Vienna, the Freudenau hydropower plant has been using the Danube's waters to produce electricity since 1998.

TOURISM

Each year, millions of tourists flock to Austria to enjoy its scenic beauty and cultural activities. Tourists often head to Vienna to meander the old **imperial** corridors of Schönbrunn Palace. They visit the city's many museums and galleries, including the Kunsthistorisches Museum, to view their artifacts and artworks.

For classical music lovers, Austria is the place to be. During the 18th and 19th centuries, some of the world's best-known composers lived there. Each year, the Salzburg Festival pays homage to Austria's rich musical tradition. It is a lavish affair with some 200 theatrical, classical, and operatic productions. The festival is held from late July to the end of August.

The Salzburg Festival is one of the world's biggest cultural festivals. More than 250,000 people attend its performances every year.

Originally built as a hunting lodge, Schönbrunn Palace later became the royal family's summer palace. Only 40 of its 1,441 rooms are open to tourists.

Austria has many attractions for those who love the outdoors. Tourists often come to Austria to hike. Trails run through forests and along mountainsides. Some pass by majestic waterfalls, such as the Krimml. Climbers often head to the country's many glaciers, including the Kitzsteinhorn in Zell am See-Kaprun, to test their skills.

Other tourists are more daring. They come to visit Austria's many ice caves, especially the Eisriesenwelt, the largest in the world. Its limestone chambers and passageways have been sculpted slowly, one drip at a time, over millions of years.

Whether downhill or cross-country, very few places can compete with Austria when it comes to skiing. The country is home to picturesque resorts, each framed by high alpine peaks. Many of these resorts have grown around farming villages. Beginners will often travel to Alpbach, one of Austria's prettiest villages. Intermediates and experts ski more challenging locales.

One of the reasons Austria is such a tourist mecca is that the country puts great effort into preserving its environment. Nearly 27 percent of its land is protected by law. Austria has seven national parks, fifty nature parks, seven **biosphere** reserves, as well as many other natural areas.

1920 First year the Salzburg Festival was held.

11,286 Height in feet of Pitztal Glacier, Austria's highest ski resort. (3,440 m)

44.8 million
Number of people who visited Austria in 2018.

People can climb to the 10,503-foot (3,201-m) Kitzsteinhorn summit on their own or with a professional guide.

INDUSTRY

Austria is one of the world's most highly developed **industrialized** countries. It is also one of the richest and most stable nations in the **European Union (EU)**. In 2018, the country had a **gross domestic product (GDP)** of about $416.6 billion. Industrial activity plays a key role in this success.

About one quarter of Austria's workers labor in manufacturing. A variety of products are made in the country. Machinery, vehicle, and steel production are the nation's top industries. Chemicals, textiles, and electronics also contribute substantially to the Austrian **economy**.

Although agriculture is still important, it plays a much smaller role in the Austrian economy than it once did. Only about 16 percent of Austria's land is suitable for farming. However, the country is home to 165,000 farms. Crops grown include wheat, barley, sugar beets, and corn. Some farmers raise livestock, such as sheep and cattle.

1% Approximate contribution of agriculture to the Austrian GDP.

More than 20,000 Number of organic farms in Austria.

$26 BILLION Amount generated by Austria's machinery production industry.

Austria's alpine environment helps companies such as Atomic Ski thrive. Based in Altenmarkt im Pongau, it has been making equipment for skiing enthusiasts since 1955.

GOODS AND SERVICES

Service industries make up the largest portion of Austria's economy. Workers in these industries provide services to others instead of producing goods. Bankers, nurses, chefs, and government employees are all examples of services workers. In Austria, the top service industries include banking, insurance, retail, government, and tourism.

Tourism is the country's top industry. In 2017, it contributed $62 billion to Austria's economy. This was about 15 percent of the country's GDP. More than 271,000 people work in Austria's tourism industry. They include tour guides, ski instructors, and restaurant chefs.

Austria trades with many nations. In 2017, it **exported** $168 billion worth of goods to other countries. Germany is its largest trading partner, receiving about 30 percent of all Austrian exports. Other key export customers are Italy, the United States, and France. Products exported include machinery, computers, iron, steel, and plastic.

The country also **imports** goods. Vehicles, chemicals, and metal goods are among the top imported products. These come mainly from other EU countries. However, Switzerland and China are also important suppliers.

$11.7 billion
Cost of goods exported from Austria to the United States in 2017.

12th Rank of Austria's economy within the EU.

74.1 Percentage of Austria's labor force working in service industries.

1995 Year Austria joined the EU.

Almost 40 million tons (36.3 million metric tons) of goods are carried along the Danube and its tributaries every year.

INDIGENOUS PEOPLES

S cientists believe that humans first came to what is now Austria about 250,000 years ago. **Archaeologists** have found the remains of these early humans in caves in and around the town of Krems an der Donau. Stone tools and cave paintings have also been found.

These early Austrians were **nomadic** hunters. They followed herds of animals in order to survive. Life was not easy, but they did find time to paint, make jewelry, and create music. About 10,000 years ago, these **Stone Age** dwellers learned to farm. As a result, people began to settle in villages and grow crops.

Celtic tribes invaded the eastern Alps in about 400 BC. They founded the kingdom of Noricum. By the 1st century BC, Noricum had become an important trading partner to the Romans. The Celtic kingdom was gradually absorbed by the Romans, who conquered the region in 15 BC. For 500 years, the Romans ruled, establishing numerous settlements. When their empire collapsed in about 400 AD, a series of Germanic tribes descended on Austria and began to build settlements of their own.

The remains of the Roman settlement of Carnuntum offer visitors a glimpse into life during the Roman occupation.

THE RISE OF THE HABSBURGS

The Rise of the Habsburgs BY THE NUMBERS

In 976, the Babenbergs, a family of German nobles, began governing Austria. The region began to flourish under their leadership, and they were given even more lands to manage. Austria grew in size as a result. Babenburg rule came to an end in 1246, however, when the last leader was killed in battle.

By the end of the 1200s, a new family, the Habsburgs, had been put in charge of Austria. Like the Babenbergs, they worked to expand the territory they governed. By the 1450s, the Habsburgs ruled not only Austria, but the entire **Holy Roman Empire** as well. They would rule this territory for more than 350 years.

Through marriage, the Habsburgs continued to expand their empire. In 1477, for example, Emperor Maximilian I married Mary of Burgundy, giving him control of present-day Belgium, the Netherlands, and Luxembourg, along with parts of northern France. Maximilian's son, Philip, married the heiress to the Spanish thrones of Castile and Aragon. When Philip's son, Charles V, inherited the throne of Spain in 1519, he immediately became ruler of more territory than any previous European monarch.

1156 Year that Austria was elevated to the status of German **duchy**.

750 Number of years the Habsburgs ruled Austria.

1191 Year Austria's national flag, one of the world's oldest flags still in use, was created.

King Rudolf I of Germany gained possession of Austria in 1278, becoming the first Habsburg to rule the country.

A CHANGING EMPIRE

In 1522, Charles V decided to divide his kingdom into two separate empires. Charles maintained control of Spain, Italy, and the lowland countries of Europe, along with Spain's American colonies. He gave his Austrian lands to his younger brother, Ferdinand.

The two brothers continued to add more territory to their empires. When Charles died in 1558, his Spanish lands were passed to his son, Philip. Ferdinand maintained control of the Austrian lands and also became Holy Roman Emperor. When he died in 1564, the Austrian empire was divided among his three sons. However, by 1620, the lands were once again under the rule of one Habsburg, Ferdinand II.

Besides being Holy Roman Emperor, Ferdinand I was also king of Bohemia and Hungary.

A firm believer in the Roman Catholic faith, Ferdinand II began to force his beliefs on his subjects. This led to a conflict known as the Thirty Years' War. Lasting from 1618 to 1648, it ended with the Habsburgs losing much of their power. Over time, however, they were able to acquire more lands and become a dominant force once again.

The Bohemian Revolt was one of the first events of the Thirty Years' War. It saw the Bohemian nobility rebel against Ferdinand II's religious views and form alliances with Protestant states.

By the mid-1700s, Austria had a new ruler, Maria Theresa. She, along with her son, Joseph II, reformed Austria and created a modern government. When the **French Revolution** broke out in 1789, Austria found itself at war with France. This conflict, combined with the country's later involvement in the **Napoleonic Wars**, led to the dismantling of the Holy Roman Empire that Austria had long dominated.

In 1848, a revolution erupted across Austrian territory. It became clear that Austria had to deal with the **nationalistic** feelings of the many different peoples that it ruled, especially the Hungarians. In 1867, Austrian ruler Francis Joseph signed the Great Compromise. It gave Hungary equal status with Austria in a new dual monarchy called Austria-Hungary.

As the years passed, tensions among various ethnic groups in the Austro-Hungarian Empire boiled over. In 1914, a Serbian nationalist assassinated Archduke Franz Ferdinand, the heir to the Austro-Hungarian throne. The murder led to World War I. Austria-Hungary, along with its German allies, lost the war. In its aftermath, the Austro-Hungarian Empire was eradicated, and the Republic of Austria was born.

A Hungary **Empire** BY THE **NUMBERS**

1.5 million
Area in square miles that Charles V ruled when he assumed control of the Habsburg Empire. (3.9 million sq. km)

8 MILLION
Approximate number of people who died during the Thirty Years' War.

23 years old
Age of Maria Theresa when she became ruler of Austria.

Archduke Franz Ferdinand and his wife, Sophie, were assassinated during a trip to Sarajevo, the capital of Bosnia and Herzegovina.

POPULATION

More than 8.7 million people live in Austria. With 42 percent of its population between the ages of 25 and 43, it is considered to be a youthful country. The northern and eastern parts of Austria are its most populous regions. The majority of people live in **urban** areas, especially Vienna.

Austrians have a good quality of life. The average Austrian can expect to live 81.6 years. Women live longer than men, at an average of 84.4 years compared to 78.9 years of age.

Austria's **migrant** population has grown in recent years. In 2016, approximately 1.89 million people in Austria had a foreign background. Most migrants are from other EU nations. Germans make up the largest subgroup, followed by Hungarians and Romanians. Immigrants from non-EU countries have arrived mainly from Afghanistan and Syria.

58.3 Percentage of Austrians living in cities.

87,675 Number of babies born in Austria in 2016.

99% Portion of the Austrian population that can read and write.

The Austrian population is evenly split between men and women. Females make up 51 percent of the entire population.

POLITICS AND GOVERNMENT

2017 Year 31-year-old Sebastian Kurz was elected Austria's chancellor, becoming Europe's youngest leader.

16 Age Austrians can begin voting.

9 Number of political parties in Austria.

Austria is a federal republic, with three branches of government. The executive branch includes a president, a chancellor, and a **cabinet** of ministers. The president is the head of state. The chancellor is the head of the government and the leader of the cabinet. The executive branch is responsible for enforcing the laws passed by the legislative branch.

The legislative branch is divided into a National Council and a Federal Council. The National Council is made up of 183 representatives elected by the people. The Federal Council has 61 members. They are elected by provincial legislatures. Austria is made up of nine states, or provinces. Each has its own governor and legislature.

Austria's judicial branch is made up of district-level courts and regional-level courts. There is an **appellate** court for the entire country, and a Supreme Court, which has the final say in all appeals. The **Constitutional** Court considers cases that involve Austria's constitution.

Austria's Parliament building is located in Vienna on a grand, horseshoe-shaped boulevard known as the Ringstrasse. The building was constructed in the late 1800s.

CULTURAL GROUPS

Today, Austria is home to people from a range of cultural and ethnic backgrounds. Some groups reflect Austria's past, when the Austro-Hungarian Empire covered much of Europe. Other groups are relatively new to the country, drawn to its prosperity and quality of life.

Most of the country's citizens identify themselves as Austrian. Called Ethnic Austrians, their culture has strong German influences. All Ethnic Austrians speak German, for instance, and it remains the country's official language. Most Ethnic Austrians practice Roman Catholicism, another nod to the country's past.

The German language can be seen on signage throughout Austria.

Villach is one of the many Austrian towns that hold festivals celebrating traditional Austrian culture. One of the highlights of the Villacher Kirchtag festival is the costume parade, which sees people in traditional dress walk through the town's main street.

The Austrian government recognizes several indigenous ethnic minorities. The Croats, Slovenes, Hungarians, Czechs, Slovaks, and Roma have special status within the country. They receive the same rights as any other Austrian citizen, but are also granted special language rights and are encouraged to maintain their traditional culture. Some of their languages, such as Croatian, Hungarian, and Slovene, have official status in parts of the country.

Perhaps no Austrian city reflects this diversity of cultural heritage better than Vienna. Nearly one third of Vienna's population is originally from another country. The majority have moved to Vienna from Serbia, Turkey, or Germany. Other immigrants have come to Vienna from Macedonia, Iran, China, Bosnia and Herzegovina, and Poland.

In recent years, Austria has become a landing spot for refugees from war-ravaged Syria. It is estimated that 50,000 Syrians are now living in the country.

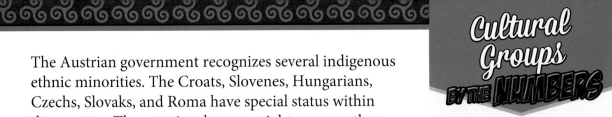

1.8 Percentage of Austrians that speak Turkish.

1.5% Portion of the Austrian population that are indigenous ethnic minorities.

3/4 Approximate portion of Austrians that are Roman Catholic.

ARTS AND ENTERTAINMENT

For many people, Austria is synonymous with great music. Some of the world's best-known classical composers made their homes there. Wolfgang Amadeus Mozart hailed from Salzburg. Joseph Haydn came from the village of Rohrau. Franz Schubert was born near Vienna. Between 1730 and 1830, these musicians, and others, composed some of the most beautiful music the world has ever heard. Their works, and those of Johann Strauss, Gustav Mahler, and Anton Bruckner, continue to be performed in concert halls and opera houses around the world.

Schubert's music is a bridge between classical and romantic music. It is known for its lyrical quality.

Classical music is also the focus of the Vienna Boys Choir. Formed hundreds of years ago, the full choir features more than 100 boys, ages 9 to 14. The choir is known for its pure, angelic sound. In fact, it was formed to sing during services at Vienna's Imperial Chapel, a tradition it continues to this day. The choir is also in demand around the world. Separated into four touring groups, the boys perform in about 300 concerts every year.

The Vienna Boys Choir often performs with the Vienna Philharmonic Orchestra at its New Year's Concert.

Austria has produced many well-known artists over the years. The best known is Gustav Klimt, a **symbolist** painter born in Baumgarten in 1862. His works are shown in galleries around the world. Today, Austrian artists continue to develop thought-provoking works. Heimo Zobernig uses videography and photography to create his art. Sculptor Erwin Wurm is best known for adding humor to his work. Xenia Hausner uses her talent to paint strong female figures.

Austrian actors have had a major impact on the world stage. Arnold Schwarzenegger is known for action movies such as *The Terminator* and *Predator*. Christoph Waltz received two Academy Awards. Klaus Maria Brandauer is best known for his role in the blockbuster *Out of Africa*.

MORE THAN 600
Number of works Mozart composed during his lifetime.

1498 Year the Vienna Boys Choir was founded.

2003 Year Arnold Schwarzenegger became governor of California.

Besides action films, Arnold Schwarzenegger also starred in several comedies, including *Jingle All the Way*, which was released in 1996.

SPORTS

With the Alps covering much of the country, it is not surprising that skiing is popular in Austria. From Benjamin Raich to Marcel Hirscher to Anna Fenninger Veith, Austria has turned out more than its share of world-class skiers. Austria has had the top alpine skiing and ski jumping team for years. They have dominated not only the Winter Olympics, but various world championships as well.

In 2019, Marcel Hirscher skied to his eighth consecutive overall World Cup title.

Among Austria's greatest skiers is Franz Klammer, who specialized in the downhill event. Born in 1953, Klammer won 25 World Cup downhill races and the gold medal at the 1976 Olympics in Innsbruck. Hermann Maier, another downhill great, won two gold medals during the 1998 Olympic Winter Games and one silver medal in 2006. He retired in 2009 after severely injuring his knee.

Anna Gasser is one of Austria's best-known snowboarders. She won the gold medal in the Big Air event at the PyeongChang Winter Olympics in 2018.

Before he became an actor and politician, Arnold Schwarzenegger was a bodybuilder. Schwarzenegger was only 20 years old when he won the Mr. Universe competition. He then went on to win seven Mr. Olympia titles. The Arnold Sports Festival, held every year in Columbus, Ohio, is named after him. It is considered one of the world's most prestigious bodybuilding events.

While its successes have been few in recent years, Austria's soccer team has a loyal following. Much of this is due to the team's past. Austria's national team was a European power in the 1930s. Most consider Matthias Sindelar to be the country's greatest soccer player. He was the star of the so-called *Wunderteam*, which won 14 straight games from 1931 to 1932. His thoughtful, complex style of play, along with his dazzling dribbling skills, made Sindelar one of the most beloved Austrian athletes of all time.

Sports BY THE NUMBERS

218 Number of medals won by Austria in all the Winter Olympics combined.

64 Miles per hour Franz Klammer averaged during his breathtaking downhill run at the 1976 Winter Olympics. (103 km per hour)

7 Number of World Cups Austria's soccer team has played in.

Austria's national soccer team plays its home games in Ernst-Happel-Stadion, in Vienna. It is the largest football stadium in the country.

Mapping Austria

W e use many tools to interpret maps and to understand the locations of features such as cities, states, lakes, and rivers. The map below has many tools to help interpret information on Austria.

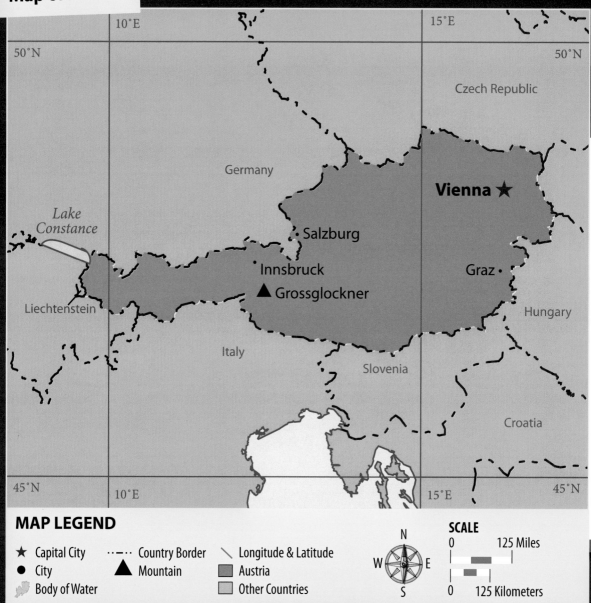

Map of Austria

Czech Republic

Germany

Vienna ★

Lake Constance

Salzburg

Innsbruck
▲ Grossglockner

Graz

Liechtenstein

Italy

Hungary

Slovenia

Croatia

MAP LEGEND

★ Capital City
● City
🌊 Body of Water

┄┄ Country Border
▲ Mountain
▨ Austria
☐ Other Countries

╲ Longitude & Latitude

SCALE

0   125 Miles

0   125 Kilometers

N
W E
S

Mapping Tools

- The compass rose shows north, south, east, and west. The points in-between represent northeast, northwest, southeast, and southwest.

- The map scale shows that the distances on a map represent much longer distances in real life. If you measure the distance between objects on a map, you can use the map scale to calculate the actual distance in miles or kilometers between those two points.

- The lines of latitude and longitude are long lines that appear on maps. The lines of latitude run east to west and measure how far north or south of the equator a place is located. The lines of longitude run north to south and measure how far east or west of the Prime Meridian a place is located. A location on a map can be found by using the two numbers where latitude and longitude meet. This number is called a coordinate and is written using degrees and direction. For example, the city of Vienna would be found at 48°N and 16°E on a map.

Map It!

Using the map and the appropriate tools, complete the activities below.

Locating with latitude and longitude
1. Which city is located at 48°N and 13°E?
2. Which mountain is located at 47°N and 13°E?
3. Which body of water is found at 47°N and 9°E?

Distances between points
4. Using the map scale and a ruler, calculate the approximate length of Austria from its border with Liechtenstein to its border with Hungary.
5. Using the map scale and a ruler, calculate the approximate distance between Innsbruck and the Grossglockner.
6. Using the map scale and a ruler, calculate the approximate distance between Graz and Austria's border with Slovenia.

Quiz Time

Test your knowledge of Austria by answering these questions.

1 What is the capital of Austria?

2 Which countries border Austria to the north?

3 What is the official language of Austria?

4 Which religion do most Austrians follow?

5 Who acts as Austria's head of state?

6 What is the EU?

7 In which year did a revolution sweep across Austria's empire?

8 In which year was the Great Compromise signed?

9 Which country formed the dual monarchy with Austria?

10 What is the population of Austria?

Key Words

appellate: relating to appeals

archaeologists: scientists who study human history by examining objects from ancient civilizations

biosphere: environmental regions occupied by living organisms

cabinet: in government, a group of senior ministers responsible for enacting government policies

Celtic: of an ancient European people who are related to the Irish, Scots, Welsh, and Bretons

constitutional: relating to a written document stating a country's basic principles and laws

duchy: the territory of a duke or duchess

economy: the wealth or resources of a country in which goods and services are produced and consumed

empire: a group of nations or territories headed by a single ruler

European Union (EU): a political and economic organization, established in 1993, that has more than two dozen member countries

exported: goods sold and sent to other countries

French Revolution: a period of time in the late 1700s that saw the people of France overthrow the monarchy and take control of the government

geologists: scientists who study how Earth formed

glaciers: large masses of moving ice

gross domestic product (GDP): the total value of goods and services produced in a country or area

Holy Roman Empire: a complex system of territories in Central Europe that developed in the Middle Ages and continued until its collapse in 1806

hydroelectricity: electricity produced using the energy of moving water, such as in a river

imperial: relating to an empire

imports: buys goods from other countries

industrialized: having many businesses and factories involved in producing goods

migrant: someone who moves from one area to another

Napoleonic Wars: a series of conflicts between the French Empire, led by Napoleon Bonaparte, and its allies

nationalistic: expressing a strong identification with one's nation and interests, especially to the exclusion or damage of other nations

nomadic: moving from place to place without a permanent home

republic: a form of government in which the head of state is elected

Stone Age: period in prehistory during which humans made weapons and tools out of stone, bone, or wood

symbolist: someone who suggests ideas through symbols

urban: relating to city life

Index

Log on to www.av2books.com

AV² by Weigl brings you media enhanced books that support active learning. Go to www.av2books.com, and enter the special code found on page 2 of this book. You will gain access to enriched and enhanced content that supplements and complements this book. Content includes video, audio, weblinks, quizzes, a slideshow, and activities.

AV² Online Navigation

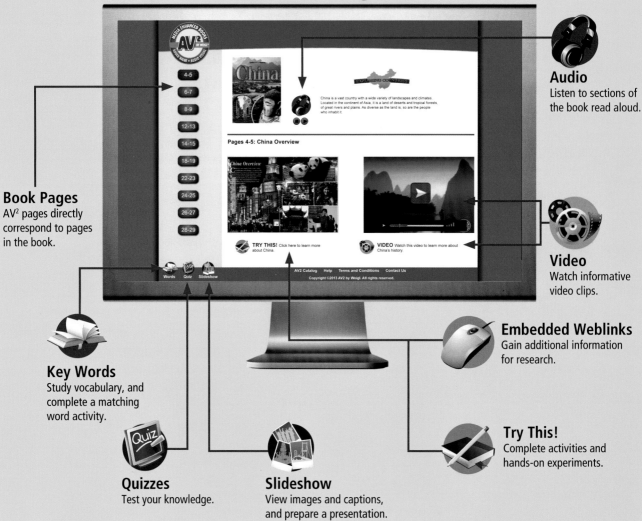

Audio
Listen to sections of the book read aloud.

Book Pages
AV² pages directly correspond to pages in the book.

Video
Watch informative video clips.

Key Words
Study vocabulary, and complete a matching word activity.

Embedded Weblinks
Gain additional information for research.

Try This!
Complete activities and hands-on experiments.

Quizzes
Test your knowledge.

Slideshow
View images and captions, and prepare a presentation.

AV² was built to bridge the gap between print and digital. We encourage you to tell us what you like and what you want to see in the future.

Sign up to be an AV² Ambassador at www.av2books.com/ambassador.

Due to the dynamic nature of the internet, some of the URLs and activities provided as part of AV² by Weigl may have changed or ceased to exist. AV² by Weigl accepts no responsibility for any such changes. All media enhanced books are regularly monitored to update addresses and sites in a timely manner. Contact AV² by Weigl at 1-866-649-3445 or av2books@weigl.com with any questions, comments, or feedback.